D0719527

000000544769

This LADYBIRD TALE
belongs to

....

DUDLEY PUBLIC LIBRARIES	
000000544769	
Bertrams	13/09/2012
SR	£4.99
	WG

Sleeping Beauty

Retold by Vera Southgate M.A., B.COM
with illustrations by Livia Coloji

LADYBIRD 🐞 TALES

ONCE UPON A TIME there lived a king and queen who were very happy, except for one thing. They both longed to have children but they had none.

Now it happened one day, when the queen had been bathing, that a frog crept out of the water and spoke to her. It said, "My Queen, before a year has gone by, you shall have a daughter."

The queen was delighted and she hurried to tell her husband the good news.

Within the year, it happened as the frog had said. A baby daughter was born to the king and queen and they were filled with joy. The child was so pretty that everyone who came to see her cried, "What a beautiful baby!"

The king was so proud of his baby daughter that he ordered a wonderful christening feast to be prepared.

The king invited all his friends to the feast, as well as kings, queens, princes and princesses from other kingdoms.

Some good fairies lived in the land and the king wanted them to be godmothers to his daughter. Now, there were thirteen fairies in his kingdom, but one was very old and no one had seen her for many years. As the king only had twelve golden plates, he invited just twelve of the fairies to come to the christening feast. The old fairy was not invited.

When the christening feast was over, the good fairies went up to the princess to give her their magic gifts.

The first fairy said, "You shall have a beautiful face."

The second fairy said, "You shall think beautiful thoughts."

The third fairy said, "You shall be kind and loving."

The fourth fairy said, "You shall dance like a fairy."

The fifth fairy said, "You shall sing like a nightingale."

When eleven of the fairies had given their gifts, the baby had been promised everything in the world one could wish for.

At that moment, the thirteenth fairy arrived. She was furious that the king had not invited her to the feast. Pointing to the baby, she cried in a loud voice, "When the king's daughter is fifteen years old, she shall prick herself with a spindle and fall down dead."

Without another word she rushed out of the palace.

All the people at the christening feast were silent with horror when they heard the words of the wicked fairy. The queen began to cry and the king did not know how to comfort her.

Then the twelfth good fairy, who had not yet given the baby her gift, stepped forward.

"Do not weep, dear Queen!" she said. "I shall do what I can to help. I cannot undo the evil spell, but I can soften it a little."

As time went by, the baby princess grew into a lovely girl. All the gifts that the good fairies had promised were hers.

She had a beautiful face and she thought beautiful thoughts. She danced like a fairy and she sang like a nightingale. She was happy, kind and loving, so that all who knew her loved her.

The king and queen loved their daughter greatly.

Now it happened that on the very day when the princess was fifteen years old, the king and queen were not at home.

To amuse herself, the girl wandered all over the palace. She opened the doors of dozens of rooms that she had never seen before.

At last she came to an old tower. She climbed up the narrow, winding staircase and found a little door at the top. She turned the rusty key in the lock and the door opened.

There, in a little room, sat an old woman at her spinning wheel busily spinning flax.

"Good day, good dame," said the princess. "What are you doing?"

"I am spinning, my child," replied the old woman.

"Oh, how wonderful!" cried the princess. "Please let me try."

No sooner had the princess touched the spindle than the fairy's wicked words came true. She pricked her finger.

As soon as she felt the prick of the spindle the princess fell upon the bed in a deep sleep.

The old woman fell asleep in her chair. And every other living creature within the palace also fell asleep.

At that very moment, the king and queen returned home for their daughter's birthday. They fell asleep in the great hall of the palace. The lords and ladies who were with them fell asleep nearby.

In the stables, the horses fell
asleep. In the courtyard, the dogs
stopped barking and fell asleep.
On the roof, the pigeons stopped
cooing and fell asleep. On the
palace walls, the flies stopped
crawling and fell asleep.

In the kitchen, the fire died out
and the meat stopped cooking.
The cook fell asleep and so
did the scullery boy.

The whole palace became silent.
Not a living creature moved.
The wind dropped and, on the
trees in the palace garden, not
a leaf stirred.

A hedge of thorns sprang up
around the palace and its gardens.
Every year, the hedge grew higher
and higher and thicker and thicker.
At last it grew so tall that it almost
hid the palace. Only the topmost
towers could be seen above it.

The story of the beautiful princess
who lay asleep spread throughout
the kingdom and far beyond. She
became known as Sleeping Beauty.

From time to time, many princes journeyed to the palace hoping to awaken Sleeping Beauty. But the thorn hedge grew so thickly that none of the princes could force his way through it.

After many years, a very handsome prince visited the kingdom. An old man told this prince the tale of Sleeping Beauty.

When the prince heard the old man's tale, he said, "I must see this beautiful princess and try to awaken her."

Now it happened that the very day on which the prince arrived was exactly one hundred years after Sleeping Beauty had fallen asleep. The evil spell of the wicked fairy had come to its end.

As the prince began to push against the hedge of thorns, every thorn turned into a lovely rose. The hedge opened of its own accord to let him pass through. And, as he passed, the hedge of roses gently closed again behind him.

The prince was spellbound as he made his way right through the flowering hedge.

At last he came to the courtyard of the palace, where the dogs lay sleeping. The prince wandered into the stables and there he found the horses all standing asleep.

Not a sound was to be heard in the whole of the palace.

Next, the prince went into the palace kitchen. The cook and the kitchen maid stood asleep. The fire was out and the meat was half cooked.

The prince walked further into the silent palace. There the king and queen sat asleep on their thrones. All was so quiet that the prince felt he should walk on tiptoes.

The prince wandered along the corridors. He looked in all the rooms he could find, but nowhere did he see Sleeping Beauty.

At length the prince came to the foot of the highest tower. He began to climb the narrow, winding staircase. When he reached the door at the top, he pushed it gently open and stepped into a small room.

There, on the bed sleeping, lay the most beautiful maiden he had ever seen.

For a long time, he looked at her in wonder, then he bent over and gave her a kiss.

At that moment, Sleeping Beauty opened her eyes and gave the prince a wonderful smile. Then she sat up, quite wide awake.

The prince gave her his hand and she stood up. Together they went down the narrow, winding staircase, along the corridors, down the main staircase, and into the great hall.

At that moment, the king and queen awoke from their sleep. They were overjoyed to see their daughter awake and well, and they welcomed the prince who had broken the spell.

Then the lords and ladies in the great hall awakened, and the whole palace began to stir.

In the kitchen, the fire began to burn and the meat began to cook.

In the courtyard, the dogs awakened and began to bark. In the stables, the horses were stirring and the pigeons on the roof awakened and flew away.

The palace had come to life again after its sleep of one hundred years. Everyone in the palace was both astonished and delighted.

Around the palace, the high hedge of thorns vanished.

A wonderful wedding feast was prepared. The handsome prince was married to Sleeping Beauty and they lived happily ever after.

A History of Sleeping Beauty

Sleeping Beauty has inspired countless picture books, films and ballets including Tchaikovsky's ballet and the triumphant 1959 Walt Disney animated film.

Sleeping Beauty's story began in the 14th century Catalan tale *Frayre de Joy e Sor de Placer*. She appears again in the 16th century French romance *Perceforest*. But it wasn't until 1697 that the title *Sleeping Beauty* was first used by Charles Perrault in his tale *La Belle au Bois Dormant* from the *Histoires ou Contes du Temps Passé (Stories or Tales of Times Past)*.

The kiss was introduced by the Brothers Grimm in their collection *Children's and Household Tales*, first published in 1812. In this version of the tale, Sleeping Beauty is called Briar Rose. Since then, many fairy tale adaptations have used this version of *Sleeping Beauty* as their source.

Ladybird's 1967 retelling of *Sleeping Beauty*, told by Vera Southgate, helped to bring the story to a new generation.

Collect more fantastic

LADYBIRD 🐞 TALES

Little Red
Riding Hood

9781409311126

Goldilocks
and the
Three Bears

9781409311119

Cinderella

9781409311072

Jack
and the
Beanstalk

9781409311102

The
Gingerbread
Man

9781409311096

The Three
Little Pigs

9781409311089

The Three Billy
Goats Gruff

9781409311065

Hansel
and Gretel

9781409311133

Puss in Boots

9781409311225

Rapunzel

9781409311195

Rumpelstiltskin

9781409311164

The Elves and the
Shoemaker

9781409311188

Snow White
and the
Seven Dwarfs

9781409311171

The
Enormous
Turnip

9781409311218

The Magic
Porridge Pot

9781409311201

Sleeping
Beauty

9781409311157

Endpapers taken from series 606d,
first published in 1964

A catalogue record for this book is available from the British Library

Published by Ladybird Books Ltd
80 Strand London WC2R 0RL
A Penguin Company

001 – 10 9 8 7 6 5 4 3 2 1

© Ladybird Books Ltd MMXII

LADYBIRD and the device of a Ladybird are trademarks of Ladybird Books Ltd

All rights reserved. No part of this publication may be reproduced,
stored in a retrieval system, or transmitted in any form or by any means,
electronic, mechanical, photocopying, recording or otherwise,
without the prior consent of the copyright owner.

ISBN: 978-1-40931-115-7

Printed in China